CONTENTS

CHAPTER I

POINT A

The bus moaned beneath him like a wounded animal. Lance Avery shifted in his seat, long legs cramped behind the cracked dashboard, one boot pressing steady on the gas pedal. Four hours behind the wheel. Thirty minutes left. A metal coffin on wheels, wheezing toward Gateway City through the fervor and haze of late summer.

The air inside was thick—sour with sweat, fried snacks, and something darker. Organic. Sour. Like rot, like shit. Lance no longer winced. He'd gone nose-blind a hundred miles back.

In the rearview mirror, all he saw were slumped bodies and slack jaws. Passengers sleeping, chewing, breathing. Meat, he thought. Nothing but meat in a long steel casing, head to tail, Point A to Point B.

A voice sliced through the static hum of tires, gripping the hot asphalt. "Good gosh, baby—where did you get this bus?" Flip McCracken clambered forward, magazine in hand. "Man, I tell you the truth—it flat-out stinks in here." Lance didn't turn. "Yeah. I know. So does the job."

Flip laughed, low and easy. "Hell, at least you still got one. You didn't use to talk like this." Lance's hands flexed, knuckles pale on the wheel. "It was that goddamn strike. You weren't here." He said "I moved down to El Paso five years ago, now?" Flip answered. "Yeah," Lance muttered. "Five years? Has it been that long?" "Sounds about right," Flip says.

Lance's jaw locked so hard the molars squealed. A dark vein throbbed along the side of his neck. Saliva gathered, bitter, metallic. Lance turned.

"They broke us, Flip," Lance said. The voice scraped out low and cracked. A humorless bark cut through his throat. He spat the rest out like a curse. "They broke us. Said we were dumb, overpaid, lazy. They took more than money. They took our pride."

Wind rattled the bus window. The sound tugged at something deep in Lance's chest.

For a moment he was back at the terminal.

January cold gnawed at his knuckles as he gripped the picket sigh. Snow soaked the cardboard until the ink began to bleed.

UNION STRONG. FAIR CONTRACT NOW.

The words ran togeather in gray streaks.

Across the driveway, a line of buses rolled out slow and smug, each one full of strikebreakers staring straight ahead.

Black-jacketed security guards formed a crooked wall. Thick boots. Blank eyes. The kind of men who looked like they were paid to break faces.

A woman with a pink suitcase stepped between the picket signs. Heels clicked.

A man in a business coat followed. A family with a stroller.

No one slowed.

No one looked.

"Excuse me," the woman said, brushing past Lance's sign as if it were a lamppost.

The cold barely registered. What Lance remembered was the sting of it. The insult—worse. The absence. Like the whole fight had turned invisible.

Somewhere in Washington, a smiling President had lifted a finger on a television screen and nodded permission. Go ahead. Break them.

A bus crept forward through the gate

Behind the wheel sat a scab driver with a crooked grin. The engine coughed, thick and oily as the bus rolled past the line.

. Lance tightened his grip on the picket sign.

For one hot second he wanted to hurl it straight through the windshield.

The bus hit a pot hole. Lance blinked. The terminal dissolved. Heat shimmered on the highway, cars whizzed by on the highway again.

His teeth were grinding.

"They didn't have to swing a fist," Lance muttered. "

They just walked right through us." The silence stretched thin, filled only by the rhythmic roar of the engine. Flip shifted, his boots scuffing against the vinyl as he hiked himself further onto the dashboard, the plastic groaning under his weight. He stared out at the darkened horizon, his jaw tight.

"Yeah," he finally exhaled, the word heavy and flat. "Not the same job anymore."

"Not since the meat packer took over," Lance said. Flip raised an eyebrow. "The what?" "The new chairman came from the food industry. Short guy. Shorter mind. Sees buses like hot dogs—you stuff 'em with meat and ship 'em down the line." He nodded toward the mirror. "Now that's how I see it, too."

Flip turned, squinting toward the rows of sleeping passengers. "Good gosh, baby..." "They're meat," Lance said flatly. "I drive meat." Silence. Flip stood up from the dash. "Damn, man, that's cold."

"No colder than they were," Lance shot back. "They walked across our picket line like we weren't even there. Screaming at us. 'Go back to work! You make too much!' You know who saves their asses when a bus breaks down in the dead of winter? Me. Not the company. Who gives his coat to a freezing passenger? Me. Not the suits."

He shook his head. "I sat next to folks in that terminal while they cried. I helped 'em. And they helped the bear tear me apart."

Flip frowned. "What bear?" "Not a real bear. A metaphor." Lance's lips curled. "I was out in the woods, going toe-to-toe with a bear, armed with nothing but a stick, holding on. And those people? They didn't just walk away. They crept up behind me and jammed a knife into my back, then left me for the bear to finish me off." The two men stared at each other. Flip, uneasy. Lance, stone-faced.

Flip's gaze drifted toward the front seat—the one no one had touched the whole ride. A stained overnight bag sagged against the window. A woman had boarded with it. She'd climbed on slowly, muttering, her arms shaking. Her pants were torn. Her eyes were somewhere else. She hadn't left the toilet since they passed mile marker 110.

"She's been in there a long time," Flip said, wrinkling his nose. "You helped her get on the bus, though, didn't you?"

Lance shrugged. "Yeah. So what?" "Thought you said you didn't care." Said Flip "I don't." A grin touched his face, dry as dust. "Chivalry ain't dead. Just bruised."

Flip laughed, more out of discomfort than humor. "You ever see someone look that bad in public? Hair-like threads. Clothes hanging off her like she ain't eaten in days. Jesus." Lance didn't answer. "I mean—don't she have anyone? No man? No kids?"

Lance's jaw twitched. "Most women manage fine." Flip sighed, "Man, I could never let myself get that low." "You think we got control over what happens to us?" Lance said, Flip shifted, taken aback.

"I didn't ask to end up here either," Lance said. "Meat from point A to point B. That's all we are. Some are fresh cuts. Some are spoiled. Some are rotten."

CHAPTER 2

THE RAGGED WOMAN

The toilet stank of ammonia, bile, and metal. The walls sweated. Plastic peeled from the corners like scorched wallpaper. Each bump in the road jolted the hinges and sent a shudder through the tiny stall where Gwendolynn Pen sat, knees clutched to her chest, arms coiled around them, spine wedged between the trash bin and the vibrating wall.

She hadn't flushed. Couldn't. It was overflowing. The sound—the violence of it—was too much. Her breath came shallow, through her mouth. She didn't dare breathe through her nose, the smell penetrating every pore. Her head leaned forward, forehead pressed to her wrist. Somewhere below, the bottle nestled beside her foot, glinting like an oily secret.

Outside the door, voices rose and fell—low masculine tones, indifferent laughter. No one missed her. No one ever did. Gwendolynn reached slowly for her purse, pulling it onto her lap. The zipper scraped like a rasp across her nerves. Her hands trembled as she opened it.

Inside, the photograph lay folded between threadbare socks and A stained handkerchief.

She pulled it free, careful not to smudge the corners. Her thumb traced the boy's jawline, his smile, the angle of his chin. Brown skin, almond eyes, a dimple buried in the right cheek. He looked proud. College ID photo. Junior year. Pre-law. His name had been Duncan. And now it was nothing. He'd died on a morning much like this one, she remembered. A charter bus on a class trip. They'd said the driver fell asleep. Said the brakes failed. Said no one suffered. Liars!

She hadn't seen his body. Now she sat beside a shit-smeared wall, trying to reach him. Her lips moved in silence. Words without a voice. This was her first time on a bus since. Each rattle of the tires over uneven asphalt vibrated through the steel floor into her bones. The engine's hum wasn't noise—it was memory. It was the snap of the brake line. It was tires howling across concrete. It was fire and screaming. She rocked slowly, not to comfort herself, but to keep from shattering.

Someone pounded on the door. She froze. "Lady?" a man's voice barked. "You okay in there?" She couldn't answer. Another tug at the door. It rattled open an inch before she yanked it shut. The struggle stopped. Footsteps faded.

Gwendolynn stared at the door as if it might melt away. She breathed through her teeth. The mirror on her lap—small, rectangular, once part of her compact—caught her reflection. Her eyes were wet. Her mascara had run. Her lipstick smeared in one direction. She looked haunted. She smiled. Then she laughed. Then she wept.

The mirror slipped from her fingers and clattered to the floor, splitting down the middle. A fissure ran right through her face. She bent to retrieve it but paused. Let it lie. The photo, still in her lap, drew her eyes. Duncan. She whispered his name aloud. It stuck in her throat. A sob crawled up from her chest and burst from her jaw. She tried to choke it down and failed. Her body began to quake.

Outside, voices. Someone laughing. The cruel edge of youth in their tone. "...still in the John?"

"...must be having dinner with the shit!" Laughter exploded. Her breath stopped. They were talking about her. She reached for the bottle, uncapped it, and let it burn down her throat. Silence returned, heavy as wet wool. In the mirror's fractured reflection, her son's face hovered over her shoulder like a ghost she'd been chasing since the crash.

She wanted to run, but the bus wouldn't stop. She couldn't run from a moving tomb. Not until Gateway City. Not until she saw the grave. Not until she said goodbye.

CHAPTER 3

THE ROAD

Antony propped his Navy Oxford, shined to a mirror finish, on the seat in front of him and stretched like he owned the whole goddamn bus. He cracked his knuckles and yawned, his jaw snapping wide as his head turned, sniffing the air. It reeked in here—ranker than the galley after fish sticks and milk day, he thought.

"Damn," he muttered, scrunching his nose. "That head stinks." He leaned into the aisle, cupping his hands around his mouth. "Hey, driver!" he hollered. "This bus smells bad enough to gag a maggot! Jesus Christ, do something!"

The diesel engine groaned in response.

Antony smirked and turned toward Mark and Morgan, who were lounging across the aisle. Mark sat staring out the window. Morgan twirled a strand of hair around her finger and gave Antony an annoyed glance.

He grinned. "What've you two been up to while I was out? Didn't get some, did ya?" Morgan's mouth curled. "The only way you'll get any is from the thing in the toilet."

Antony barked out a laugh. Scanning the bus, he checked the passengers' reactions. No reaction. He continued, "Oh, she's still in there?" He turned, peering over the back of his seat. The restroom door stood shut. "What's she doing, having dinner in there?" He cupped his hands. His voice thundered through the bus. "Slut! Get your head out of the head! Dinner's over!"

Mark groaned and rubbed his eyes. "Knock it off." But Antony was on a roll. "Hey, Mark, why don't you go get some of that? I heard you'll cut anything—Hack Saw!" Morgan snorted. "Oooo, Antony." Mark shot them a pained look. "She's not bothering anybody."

"Yeah," Morgan purred, "but I bet you'd like to bother her." Antony leaned over. "Bet you would. Bet you want to as much as you want Morgan."

"You're sick," Mark snapped. "You're really sick."

Morgan pointed toward the bathroom with mock concern. "Why would she want Mark? She already has her 'John." Antony held his nose, eyes wide. "Yeah, a real strong John. You think he'll give her something for dinner?" He paused, milking it. "A honey bucket?"

Morgan howled with laughter.

Antony added, "No—oh no—it'll be a shit-eatin' surprise!" They cackled like feral kids in a schoolyard. Mark shifted uncomfortably, shoulders tense.

At the front, the bus mic clicked on with a metallic whine. "Gentlemen," Lance's voice crackled, annoyed, dry, and low, "please confine your conversation to your seatmate and do not speak to the whole bus."

Antony stood and threw a mock salute. "Yes, sir!"

The mic crackled again. "That's about as funny as a screen door on a submarine." The words hung in the air. A low chuckle spread through the bus. Antony froze, staring into the rearview mirror. The driver's eyes stared back—two chips of coal, flat and unmoving. He sat down, muttering under his breath. "Old bastard."

Morgan chewed her gum louder. Mark looked out the window.

Behind the bathroom door, Gwendolynn rocked in silence, one hand pressed against the inside panel. Her stomach curled inward. The voices outside still echoed. *Slut. She ain't nobody.* Each word jabbed like pins beneath her skin. She pressed the bottle to her lips.

In the driver's seat, Lance Avery adjusted the mic with a twitch of his jaw. He hadn't liked what he heard. Not one bit. The bus rattled on, and the smell didn't leave. But something in Lance had begun to shift.

CHAPTER 4

HOT AIR

Flip McCracken thumbed through his magazine for the third time without reading a word of it.

Sweat rolled down his chest beneath his shirt like a lazy insect. The air in the bus clung thick to his skin—hotter now, humid and foul, as if someone had boiled a septic tank in a slow cooker and poured it into the vents.

He coughed, fanning himself with the folded pages. "Good gosh," he muttered, glancing toward the front. "How in the hell is anybody still breathing in here?"

He slid out of his seat and made his way to the front, past Mark, who stared grimly out the window, and Morgan, who had gone quiet but still radiated perfume and venom. Antony slumped in his seat, subdued for now, though his eyes twitched with unfinished mischief.

Lance didn't look up as Flip approached

"She still in there?" Flip jerked his thumb toward the restroom door. Lance nodded, jaw tight. Flip sniffed the air, then recoiled.

"Man, that ain't right." Lance didn't answer. His fingers twitched on the steering wheel.

Flip approaches the bathroom, his hand knocking softly on the toilet door. The oppressive heat hits him harder here, where the engine's rumble seeps through the floor panels. He presses his ear to the door, listening. It vibrates faintly under his knuckles. "Hey, lady? You alright in there?"

Nothing.

He knocked again, more firmly. "Come on now. You been in there longer than a three-day layover. Some folks got to go, too." Still silence. He tugged the door open.

Flip blinked. A pale hand jerked it shut. Not forcefully. Weak. Defensive. Flip felt it more than saw it—that trembling refusal. The kind of pull you make when you have nothing left but the shame of being seen.

Flip hesitated. "Lady, you okay?" Still nothing. He stood there for a beat longer, staring at the metal seam of the door, half-expecting it to dissolve and reveal something far worse than the stench.

He gave the door one last tug, got the same response—a feeble, frightened resistance—and let it go. Sighing, he turned around and muttered, "I tell you the truth..." as he walked back toward Lance.

"She alright?" Lance asked without taking his eyes off the road.

"She's in there. That's about all I know," Flip replied. "Didn't say nothin'. Door moved, but..." He shook his head. Flip made his way down the aisle, bracing himself against the backs of the seats as the bus rocked down the road

Behind him, the toilet door creaked open. Flip turned.

She emerged, her head down, strands of hair stuck to her cheeks in dark ribbons. She walked like the floor was ice, every step cautious, fragile. Her hands gripped her overnight bag as if it were the only thing keeping her upright.

Flip stiffened.

Antony and Morgan watched her struggle down the aisle, swaying side to side to the rhythm of the bus. They flinched in exaggerated disgust, fanning their noses and scooting away like children avoiding a wet dog. Morgan whispered something sharp into Antony's ear. He laughed once—short and cruel.

Gwendolynn passed, afraid to look up.

Flip glanced at Lance. Lance's eyes were fixed on the road, his face unreadable, carved from stone by years of shutdown. Sweat rolled down his temple as he stared ahead, eyes darting left to right, checking the mirror as if daring it to blink first. They fell into a silence that wasn't quite companionable.

Gwendolynn reached the front row. Her knees gave out, and she collapsed into the seat. She stared, empty-eyed, her shoulders heaving, then slowly pulled a small mirror from her bag. She studied her reflection with the reverence of someone searching for someone long gone. Then she laughed. And cried. At the same time. A broken seesaw of emotion rocked back and forth inside her throat, and a long, hollow moan echoed through the bus.

Flip swallowed hard and looked away. "Goddamn heat's gettin' to people," he muttered. But it didn't sound right. Didn't feel like a joke anymore.

Lance didn't respond.

Gwendolynn closed her eyes. Her body relaxed, and her head leaned against the soft headrest. She began speaking to Lance, quietly at first, as if nothing had happened. "I had a son, Duncan." Flip heard her mention Gateway City, something about a college, maybe a son. He tuned it out. Too heavy. Too much. He picked up his magazine again and pretended to read. But the air on the bus had changed. It wasn't the heat. It was something else.

CHAPTER 5

CHOCKEHOLD

The mirror cracked

A spider-vein fracture ran across Gwendolynn Pen's reflection like a wound no makeup could hide. She angled the mirror left, then right, trying to see around the split. All she found were pieces of herself—eyebrows severed, lips misaligned, one eye floating above the other, as if it belonged to a stranger. She pressed the mirror closer to her face. There she was: half a woman.

The air thickened, tightening around her throat. The bus swayed with the road, a nauseating rhythm that lulled her into helpless silence. Gwendolynn stared at her reflection, her eyes stinging from the strain, yet she couldn't tear her gaze away. Her body trembled, her hands trembling against the chipped plastic frame.

It was the bus. The bus was doing this. She should never have gotten on.

Duncan's photo lay hidden in her bag, untouched since she left the restroom. She avoided looking at it now. She could feel the edge of the stiletto tucked beneath her socks, carefully wrapped in a tissue like a relic. A single slip of steel with a handle she could bite down on if necessary. She hadn't planned to bring it; it simply found its way in.

Duncan's funeral was tomorrow. She'd already missed the vigil and the eulogies. She wasn't even sure she'd be allowed at the grave.

She glances toward the back of the bus, where the girl and the sailor sit. Their eyes are like sharp razors, painted with lipstick and arrogance. She remembers the girl laughing earlier when Gwendolynn steps out of the toilet—laughing without shame, as if cruelty is the latest trend. The boy's sneer lingers in her mind, nostrils flared.

They had whispered about her. She heard her name once—or what passed for it. "John." As in toilet. As in whore.

A low snort escaped her lips before she realized it. Her mouth curled into a grin she hadn't intended.

Then she laughed.

It came out of her in a sputter, like a cough that turned into a giggle and wouldn't stop. Her shoulders twitched. Her ribs ached. The laugh crept up, pushed past her lips in sputtering bursts—until it cracked like a bottle against tile. Tears followed, hot and fast.

She rocked forward, both hands to her mouth. The mirror fell into her lap again, its crack winking in the overhead light. Someone snickered behind her.

Gwendolynn pressed her palms to her face. Breathe. Don't listen. She closed her eyes and whispered, "Don't be meat. Don't be meat."

The bus was a pressure chamber. A moving, groaning casket with walls too tight, air too thick. She clawed at her throat as if her scarf were strangling her, though she wasn't wearing one. Her pulse galloped in her ears.

"Ma'am?" the driver said, his voice distant. She didn't respond. "You okay up there?"

Gwendolynn looked up, eyes wide. Her mouth opened, but no sound came out.

She shook her head. No. She wasn't okay. She hadn't been since the phone rang, since they said he's gone, since they handed her a map to a cemetery she'd never planned to visit.

But how do you explain that to strangers? How do you explain the ache that settles under your bones and builds a nest? How do you explain that your child's body was burned in a wreck not unlike this one—that every bump, every rattle, every diesel groan is a ghost crawling up your spine?

She turns to Lance, her eyes bloodshot, her lips trembling. "Have you ever lost someone?" she asks. Lance meets her gaze in the mirror, unblinking and silent. She nods, a quiet acknowledgment. "I did," she whispers, carefully touching the crack in the mirror with her pinky. "I'm going to see him tomorrow. He's not really there, but... I have to go."

Behind her, the laughter resumed. Soft at first, then louder. "She's talking to herself again?" Morgan whispered. "Maybe she's talking to her imaginary friends," Antony chuckled.

Gwendolynn lowered the mirror. Closed her eyes. The choke-hold returned—tighter this time. A memory bloomed in the dark behind her lids. The crash. A burst of fire. Sirens. A closed casket. No goodbyes. Only silence. And silence could kill you slower than any wreck.

CHAPTER 6

THRED AND FLAM

Morgan Wright, in a slow, practiced move, crossed one long leg over the other and leaned sideways, angling her breast toward Mark. She adjusted the thin strap of her tank top with theatrical nonchalance, letting her fingers graze her collarbone like a lover's breath. Mark didn't notice. He stared out the window, watching soybeans flicker past like rows of broken teeth.

She hated it when he did that—checked out, looked away, ignored the performance. "You know," she said sweetly, "I didn't hurt you, did I, Mark?" He didn't answer. She pouted, leaned closer, and lowered her voice to a throaty whisper. "If you want to stay with me, you won't worry about her." pointing at the toilet.

Her gaze like molten lava fell on Gwendolynn's seat. "She ain't nobody," Morgan mutters. "You want to worry about her when you got me?"

Mark gave no sign he'd heard. Morgan straightened, sat tall, and arched her back like a dancer posing for a shutter click. "I'm gonna be a star when I get to California. Bet you didn't know that." Her voice danced between defiance and delusion. “You can say you had dinner with a star. I might even send you one of my pictures.”

She reached down, smoothing her skirt tightly over her thighs, then tilted her head slightly, casting a sidelong glance at Mark through her lashes. “You do want to take me to dinner, don’t you, Mark?” His response came slowly, mechanical and unconvincing. “Yeah. I want to take you out.”

Antony turned from across the aisle, a smirk playing on his lips. "You don’t have what it takes for a woman like that.” Morgan’s face lit up. "Why don’t you come over here, sailor boy? Let a real man talk to me.” Mark remained silent. Antony flexed his chest. "You got that right, baby. I’ll take good care of you."

Morgan turned, her eyes scanning him slowly from top to bottom before she sneered. “But I don’t think you will.” Her laugh was loud and short, then she pivoted back toward Mark. But his expression was guarded now—face hard, eyes narrow, mouth a tight line. That irritated her. She wanted him to desire her—to chase her, orbit her, need her. Not to look away.

Gwendolynn returned from the toilet, moving slowly, like a ghost moving through fog. She sat, mumbled to herself, and started fussing with her hair. Her mirror flickered in the light.

Morgan watched her like a condor circling roadkill. “Did you see that?” she whispered. “Did you see what she’s wearing?”

Mark didn’t respond.

“You really think she used to be somebody? College?” She giggled. “College of Crazy Bitches, maybe.”

Gwendolynn starts to speak, her words cracked and faint. "I had a son, Duncan." Morgan squints, then raises her voice enough for everyone on the bus to hear. "Hey, Miss John has a son." She pauses, then adds coldly, "Some men will sleep with anything."

Antony snorted. "If I was her son, I'd lay down in front of a bus and die." They laughed. Loud. Mean. Like middle school kids with knives.

Gwendolynn sprang to her feet. Her overnight bag thumped against her hip. Her eyes blazed—not with fire, but with something worse. Grief wrapped in fury. "STOP!" she screamed. Her whole body trembled, her voice no drained of all hope. " Please stop."

Morgan flinched. For one brief moment, she saw it: this woman had something inside her—a storm. Maybe not strength, but sorrow sharp enough to draw blood.

Gwendolynn turned, her head down, and walked to her sanctuary, the restroom. The laughter died.

Mark leaned forward, turned to Morgan, his eyes dark. "I think you belong over there with him," he said, his voice like gravel dragged across a steel plate.

Morgan blinked. "What?" "You don't want me?" she said, light and teasing. "You don't want all this?" He looked her up and down. "All what?" His gaze dropped her like a stone tossed down a well. "You're nothing but cruel fluff," he said. "There's not even a real person in there. Just make-believe."

Morgan's mouth fell open, then closed again. Cruel fluff. The words landed with surgical precision. Mark turned away.

The bus rocked. The engine howled. The sky outside had begun to bruise.

Morgan sat perfectly still. Not crying, not moving. As if motion might snap the fragile shell she'd built around herself. She didn't speak again.

CHAPTER 7

DINNER WITH A STAR

Mark Diamonds stared out the window, trying to ignore the tightness in his chest.

Outside, the flatland rolled by in slow motion—miles of nothing wrapped in heat. Telephone poles ticked past like slow seconds on a dying clock. Inside, the bus simmered. Air thick enough to bite. Stale, sweaty, sour.

Morgan sat beside him, silent, her legs crossed, her shirt pulled tight. The show had ended. There was no applause. No encore.

He hadn't meant to say it like that—cruel fluff—but he hadn't meant to lie either. She wasn't evil. Not exactly. She was afraid of being ignored. Of being ordinary. Of not being looked at.

And so she reached for the only weapon she had—beauty, weaponized like a blade. She carved people with it. Made them bleed and called it flirting. He saw it now. Saw her rehearsed smiles and honeyed voice and the desperate grip she kept on attention like it was air and she was drowning.

But that didn't excuse the way she laughed at the woman in the front seat. It didn't excuse the way she had dragged Gwendolynn through filth and piss and humiliation—and called it entertainment.

Mark's eyes shifted ahead. The woman remained still for minutes, hunched over with her mirror, whispering softly. Her hands trembled each time the wheels jostled over a seam.

A stiletto-thin shadow fell across her cheek. Mark swallowed. His mouth was dry. He thought about what Antony had said. The fake salute. The yelling. The bile. Antony had stopped smiling, too.

Mark wasn't a hero. He wasn't brave. He hadn't done a goddamn thing except look away while it all happened. While she was humiliated. While Morgan preened and smirked and poured venom with a sugar-coated spoon.

Some men will sleep with anything. He'd laughed. Not out loud, but inside. That was worse.

Mark shifted in his seat, muscles sore from sitting still too long. He reached under his jacket and pulled out a crumpled granola bar. He unwrapped it slowly, not hungry, but needing to move.

Morgan glanced sideways at the crackle of foil. "You gonna share that?" she asked, voice flat.

He looked at her. Really looked. She wore fatigue like mascara now. Her eyes were dull. Her mouth tight. She looked smaller—less starlet, more kid with bad dreams.

"No," he said. "You already ate."

Her lip twitched, but she didn't push back. Not this time.

He stared down at the granola bar, but didn't bite.

Instead, he turned in his seat, looked forward again, past Flip's hunched back and Lance's rigid posture, toward Gwendolynn.

She rocked slightly. Hair clinging to her neck. Bottle tucked out of sight in her overnight bag, but he knew it was there. Like a rosary. Like a noose.

Mark leaned forward. "You okay, ma'am?" he asked quietly. She didn't turn. Didn't acknowledge him. Maybe she didn't hear. Maybe she didn't believe. Behind him, Morgan shifted in her seat and stared out the opposite window. Mark looked down at the uneaten bar. He didn't know what it meant to be a man anymore. Not really. Not after all this. But he knew what it wasn't.

CHAPTER 8

FIRE IN THE GUT

The steering wheel buzzed beneath Lance Avery's palms like a live wire. He gripped it tighter, his knuckles white against the grainy rubber. The smell inside the bus hadn't changed—still ripe with sweat, piss, engine grease, and something sour enough to peel the lining off his throat. But that wasn't what made his stomach turn. It was the silence. Not the kind that meant peace. The kind that came after something cruel.

Morgan's voice had gone quiet. Mark hadn't said a word since he'd called her bluff. Flip was flipping pages in that damn magazine again, but he hadn't turned a page in twenty minutes. Antony... well, Antony had gone still. The swagger drained out of his posture.

Gwendolynn sat in the front seat, staring into her fractured mirror like it held a different world. One she'd fallen out of and could never get back into.

Lance glanced at her through the rearview mirror. Saw her lips move. No sound.

That did it. He snapped on the microphone. His voice cracked through the speaker, rougher than he'd intended. "No drinking on the bus," he said sharply. Gwendolynn jerked. Her fingers fumbled with the bottle she'd been cradling in her lap like a child.

"Give it to me," Lance said, leaning forward, hand out.

She hesitated. Pulled it back to her chest, clutching it like a relic. Her eyes went wild, cornered-animal wild. Panic bloomed across her face. She offered it. Pulled it back. Offered again. Her hands trembled.

He softened his tone. "Give it up or get off." That landed. She closed her eyes and passed it forward. He took it and set it on the dashboard. She stared at the windshield, her body trembling.

He shifted his gaze back to the bustling road, the roar of traffic filling his ears, yet her muffled sobs haunted him from behind. The sight of the bottle in her grip refused to fade, and the curve of her son's name lingering on her lips remained vivid in his mind. "You okay, lady?" he asked under his breath. No mic this time. No answer. He didn't expect one.

Lance shifted in his seat, feeling the anger building inside him. Memories of Flip mentioning the strike, the kids laughing at that woman as if she were a joke, all fed the fire in his gut. He found himself murmuring the word 'meat' over and over, as if it could dull his urge to give in.

She's not meat. He saw that now. She was a bag of raw, broken skin walking. A woman carrying death in her purse. A mother on the worst ride of her life. And he'd let them humiliate her.

He'd let himself believe she didn't matter because believing otherwise hurt too goddamn much. He looked up and caught her eye in the mirror for just a second. Her gaze was glassy yet aware.

Lance cleared his throat. "You're gonna be alright," he said softly. "Try to relax. Ain't much longer now."

She looked at him as if no one had spoken to her kindly in months, maybe years. That hurt more than it should've.

Lance's jaw tightened as the chuckle echoed behind him. He couldn't tell if it was Morgan or Antony, nor did he care. He snapped the mic back on. "You keep your mouth shut, or I'll kick your ass off this bus right here in the middle of one of these cornfields."

The bus fell quiet again—this time, for the right reasons.

Lance didn't look at Gwendolynn. He didn't need to. Something had changed. The fire in his belly wasn't rage anymore. It was shame. And the need to do something before it burned him clean through.

CHAPTER 9

MEAT

Flip McCracken shifted in his seat, the vinyl squeaking softly beneath him. His magazine lay in his lap, pages bent and untouched, for miles of travel.

He fixated on the narrow aisle of the bus, his gaze passing Antony sulking into the window, Morgan with her arms crossed and jaw clenched, and Mark sitting stiff and grim. His eyes reached the front row, where Gwendolynn Pen sat clutching only a mirror and the remnants of herself.

He didn't *want* to care. Not really. That wasn't his style.

Flip was the guy who made you laugh at the worst possible time. The one who cracked a joke in the emergency room or called his divorce "just another pit stop." That's how he kept the world from crawling in.

But Lance had changed. No longer smiling and easygoing. And when Lance changed, Flip felt it. Felt it like the weather turning icy cold.

He remembered a time not long ago—maybe a decade, maybe a lifetime—when Lance was the guy who'd give a kid his sandwich on a layover. Who carried extra blankets in winter. Who kept gum in the glove box in case a crying baby needed a distraction.

Now. Lance talked about passengers' "pork links in a sausage casing." *Meat from point A to point B.*

Flip had laughed when he said it—laughed like it was clever. But when he looked at Gwendolynn—slouched, shaking, muttering into her mirror like it was a telephone to someone she'd lost—it didn't sound clever anymore. It sounded like rot. *Spoiled meat.*

That's what he'd called her. Flip had said it. Joked about it. He closed his eyes and leaned back, his head resting against the window, heat bleeding through the glass. The bus jostled over a seam in the road. He felt it in his molars.

"She didn't come on this bus like no sack of garbage," Lance had said not long ago. Flip hadn't answered. He'd only nodded, maybe grunted. But now it wouldn't leave him alone.

She'd come on like a ghost—sure. Dirty. Disheveled. Probably hadn't slept indoors in weeks. She smelled like a liquor store basement. But she had something else in her bag besides cheap vodka and toilet paper. She had grief. And it filled the whole goddamn bus.

Flip opened his eyes and stared at her again. She wasn't crying now. She wasn't mumbling. She was still—like a building after a fire. Nothing left but heat in the walls. He reached for the magazine in his lap. Flipped it open. Tried to read. The words slid off the page like grease. He slammed it shut again.

"You alright, Flip?" Lance's voice crackled up from the front. "Yeah," he called back, but it didn't sound convincing. "Good gosh, baby," he muttered under his breath, shaking his head. He turned toward the window, but the reflection staring back at him wasn't a comic, wasn't a clown, wasn't a sidekick. It was a man who hadn't said a damn thing while a woman was being torn apart right in front of him.

Flip sighed. The air felt heavier. The bus kept rolling. And there were still a few miles left to change who he was before they reached the end of this hellish journey.

CHAPTER 10

MIRROR TALK

The mirror trembled in Gwendolynn Pen's hand, catching slivers of sunlight as the bus weaved through Illinois farmland. It flashed like a signal, though she wasn't sure who it was signaling to anymore. Herself, perhaps. Or the version of herself who still mattered.

The crack in the glass had widened. A jagged line slicing her face into two mismatched halves. She tilted it gently. One side showed her mouth, creased and drawn. The other caught a faded piece of her eye. The rest was distortion, fragments. She studied them anyway.

"Still here," she whispered. "Still breathing." Though she wasn't sure why. The bottle was gone. The driver—Lance, she remembered—had taken it. Not roughly, not cruelly. He'd asked. Demanded, but in a way that made her think, maybe, just maybe, he hadn't stopped seeing her completely. And he'd said it would be okay. She didn't believe him, but she wanted to.

The bus jolted. Her elbow hit the armrest, and she nearly dropped the mirror. She caught it clumsily, then stared down at it, her heart quickening. For a moment, the reflection blurred—and in its place, she saw Duncan. The real Duncan

Not the glossy photo. Not the smiling schoolboy. But her son as he'd last looked: tall, lanky, overwhelmed by life yet still fighting to grow into it. His hands had become those of a man. His voice had deepened. He used to call her "Ma" with a mix of tenderness and exasperation, the way young men do when they're trying not to cry in front of anyone.

"I'm going to law school," he'd said on their last phone call. "You always say that," she'd teased. "Well, this time, I mean it." She unclenched her fists, the words lingering on her tongue. Her shoulders sagged as she glanced away, exhaustion weighing her down. She believed there would be other moments, other sentences left unsaid. But then the screech of metal and shattering glass cut everything short.

She reached down into her bag and withdrew the photograph—creased, water-stained, worn soft at the edges from too much touching. It was folded in half, and she opened it delicately, like an open wound.

Duncan grinned from the page, teeth straight, hair cropped short. "Hi, baby," she murmured. "It's almost time." She blinked slowly, not yet crying. Her face ached from holding it together. But she spoke anyway. She had to. It was the only thing keeping her from falling through the floor. "I'm coming, sweetheart. I know I'm late. You probably think I forgot."

The mirror caught her lips moving. She watched herself speak, detached and hollow. "I didn't forget. I could never forget you." She traced the outline of his jawline with a fingertip. Her skin brushed the ink, just once.

"I know I look crazy. I probably smell like an alley. People are laughing. That's fine." The bottle would've helped. She missed its fire, the way it made things float. But she didn't reach for it. Couldn't. Not now. Duncan didn't need her drunk. He needed her to show up. Alive. Even if it hurts.

"I don't care if I'm turned away at the gate," she said, her resolve stronger. "I'll stand outside the damn fence all day if I have to. I'll say goodbye through the trees." The mirror trembled again.

She could hear Antony behind her, still muttering under his breath. Morgan hadn't spoken since Mark gutted her ego. Flip hadn't laughed in half an hour.

Good.

Let them sit in their silence. Let them think about what it means to be cruel.

Gwendolynn leaned her head back against the seat, the photo clutched in one hand, the mirror in the other. "I'm still your mama," she whispered. "Even if nobody else can see me anymore." For the first time all day, she let the quiet settle on her shoulders without shaking it off.

CHAPTER II

ALL THIS

Morgan Wright sat still, her posture perfect, her expression blank. It was the only control she had left. Her fingers gripped the seat beside her, nails tight against the plastic as the bus rattled across another uneven stretch of highway. The road hummed beneath her like judgment.

Mark hadn't looked at her since.

"Cruel fluff." The words looped, snagging inside her like a bad hook in a better song. She kept trying to push it away, push *him* away, but the echo lingered. You don't want all this? *All what?*

She glanced down at her legs—smooth, tan, crossed elegantly. Her hands were soft, nails shaped. Her clothes clung the right way. She'd always been told that was enough. That being wanted was the same as being *worthy*.

But it wasn't working anymore.

Mark had looked at her like she was a fake diamond in bad light. Not angry. Not even disgusted. Just tired. Like he'd finally seen through the wrapping and realized there was nothing inside but stale air. She hated that look.

She shifted in her seat, deliberately loud, hoping to draw his attention. He didn't flinch. Didn't turn. His whole body angled away from her like she was noise.

Morgan's throat tightened. She reached into her purse, pulled out her compact, and flicked it open. Her reflection blinked back, flawless on the surface. But her eyes were off. They darted too fast. Lids fluttered.

She looked scared. Like someone trying not to cry in public. That pissed her off more than anything. She wasn't supposed to care. She was supposed to *win*.

She bit her lip hard, then reapplied gloss. She checked her lashes. Blotted her face with a tissue that shook just a little too much.

Gwendolynn muttered something again, voice dry and hoarse like brittle leaves blowing across pavement.

Morgan froze.

She turned slowly in her seat, just enough to see the ragged woman in the first row. Gwendolynn's head was bowed. A photo in her lap. The cracked mirror beside it. She wasn't looking at anyone. She wasn't saying anything cruel. She was *still*. The woman she'd laughed at. Pointed at. Called names. Mark had defended *her*. Not Morgan.

Morgan turned back around, face burning—not with heat but with something colder. Guilt, maybe. Or shame. But she didn't have a name for that feeling. She'd never had to. When men didn't want her, she moved on. When girls judged her, she got skinnier, prettier, louder. This felt different. This felt like being exposed.

She crossed her arms and leaned against the window, cheek pressed to the glass, trying to cool the heat in her face. It didn't help.

The silence on the bus had changed.

No one was talking. Not even Antony. Not even Flip. And that quiet wasn't peace. It was reckoning.

Morgan swallowed hard and stared out at the endless fields of corn blurring past the windows. Green rows, yellow dust, sky like tin.

She'd thought she'd be in Los Angeles by now. She'd imagined the casting calls, the nightclub lights, the line of boys begging to say they knew her *when*.

But here she was—sweating in a seat that stuck to her skin, makeup melting, heart racing, watching her whole act crumble under the weight of a woman who didn't even *try* to be seen.

She closed the compact "Fluff." That's what he said. Morgan stared at her reflection in the window. And for once, didn't recognize the girl staring back

CHAPTER 12

THE SWITCH

Mark Diamonds sits rigid in his seat, eyes fixed on the horizon beyond the greasy window. Fields stretch endlessly past him, a sea of green beneath a sky so vast it feels hollow. Behind him, an engine hums steadily. Ahead, a woman who has faced their worst whispers softly to ghosts.

Beside him, Morgan hadn't moved. She hadn't spoken since he'd told her the truth—that she was fluff, cruel fluff.

He hadn't meant it to be cruel. But it had been honest. And that, for once, had been more important. She hadn't argued. That was the surprising part. No flash of teeth, no coy defense, no lashing back. She'd turned away like someone who'd been hit too hard to respond. Good, he thought. And then, immediately—not good. Just necessary.

He hadn't expected to feel *anything* about her pain. But there it was. It didn't bloom like guilt. It pressed on him like a weight.

He brushes his palm across his thigh, feeling the dampness beneath the white cotton. The bus was cooking slowly, reeking of urine, old food, scorched rubber, and unspoken regret.

He glanced toward the front. Gwendolynn sat perfectly still in her seat, one hand on a photograph, the other limp at her side. Her mouth moved, but he couldn't hear her. He didn't need to.

She'd stopped trying to make anyone understand. That silence screamed louder than anything Antony had ever shouted. She no longer looked crazy. She looked tired. Wrecked. Like someone walking through flames, trying not to burn.

Mark leaned forward, his voice barely above a whisper. "Ma'am?" She remained still, her shoulders betraying a slight shift, revealing she had heard him despite her unflinching stance. He nodded quietly, unsure whether she had noticed.

Behind him, Flip stood and stretched with a groan, then walked up the aisle toward the front. Antony didn't look up. His head lolled against the window. The performance had ended for him, too.

Mark felt something in his chest shift, like a door creaking open after years of being stuck. The kind of movement that doesn't make a sound but rearranges everything.

He turned toward Morgan. She was still facing the window, arms crossed, pretending not to notice him watching. "I meant what I said," he told her. Calm. Final. Her jaw tightened, but she didn't speak.

"You laughed at someone who's drowning," he added. "That's not strength. That's cowardice." Still no answer. "You think I care about your picture in L.A.? I don't. You want to be famous? Fine. But I'd rather be decent." That did it.

She turned, slowly. Her face blank, her eyes shimmered. "You think you're better than me now?" she asked. Her voice wasn't mean. It was small. "No," he said. "I think I've been worse than you for a while." He stood. Gave her one last look—not angry, not cruel. Just done.

He got up and walked past the rows of silent passengers, then sat in the row across from Gwendolynn, not beside her. Not crowding her. But near. Close enough to matter. He didn't say anything else. Didn't need to. Sometimes, doing the right thing didn't come with a speech. Sometimes it came with silence and presence. And that was the switch.

CHAPTER 13

CORNFIELD ULTIMATUM

The road narrowed, two thin lanes slicing through a cornfield corridor. The stalks pressed close on either side, as if listening. Lance Avery's grip on the wheel had turned to stone. His forearms ached. His molars throbbed from grinding. The stink inside the bus hadn't let up, but now it was more than piss and mildew. Now it was *moral rot*. The kind that stuck to your clothes.

He'd heard it—Antony's last crack, slicing through the quiet like a rusted razor. "If I was my son, I'd lay down in front of a bus and die." He didn't yell at first. Didn't even blink. He breathed in through his nose and let the fire roll up from his belly to his chest. Slow. Measured. Righteous. Lance slammed on the brakes.

The bus lurched forward. Bags shifted in the overhead racks. Flip grabbed a pole. Morgan yelped. Mark's head snapped toward the front.

Lance twisted in his seat and locked eyes with the sailor.

"You keep your mouth shut," he said, his voice like gravel dragged over steel. "Or I'll kick your ass off this bus right here—in the middle of these goddamn cornfields."

Silence swallowed the bus whole.

Antony blinked, caught off guard. Then—slowly, stupidly—stood. His uniform creased from sleep. He puffed his chest out like a drunk rooster.

"Oh yeah?" he smirked. "You and which duty section?"

Flip stood before Lance even turned. No smile now. No joke. He moved with the calm that said: Don't test me. "I'll help him if he needs it," Flip said, eyes locked on Antony. Antony's smirk started to die. Mark stood. "I'll help him too," he said, voice low but solid. Antony stared at him, stunned. "What?" Mark didn't flinch. Didn't blink. Just looked at him like a man who'd finally made up his mind. "I'm done watching you treat people like garbage."

Antony backed down and slowly slid into his seat, like a balloon losing air. His shoulders sagged. His mouth closed. No comeback. No bravado.

The cornfields outside hissed in the wind.

Morgan sat frozen, her eyes darting from one man to the next, waiting to see where the power had landed. She didn't say a word.

Lance looked into the mirror. Gwendolynn hadn't moved, but her fingers had stopped shaking.

Flip walked toward the front. His voice cracked. "Good gosh, baby… what the hell happened to us?" Lance didn't answer right away. He stared through the windshield at the endless rows of corn, the long stretch of sky. The terminal twenty minutes out.

"That lady is hurting," he said at last. "She was hiding in that damn toilet because she was scared to death. And we... all of us... We turned our noses up like she wasn't even a person."He exhaled long and hard.

"Because she looked different. Smelled different. Acted different. We pushed her into that stinking stall and let her rot there like she deserved it." Flip glanced over his shoulder at the restroom door. His throat bobbed. "In that foul toilet," Lance muttered. "With all that shit and piss..." He shook his head, eyes wet but not blinking.

"We never stopped to think maybe she had a life. A son. A reason to keep going. Maybe she needed just a little bit of goddamn respect." He looked at Flip. "We're worse than our own waste, man." Flip nodded slowly. "Yeah," he said. "Yeah, maybe we are." A long pause filled the bus. Even the engine noise seemed quieter.

Lance turned toward the restroom. "I'm gonna try to help her," he said. "When we get to Gateway City, I'll be there for her." Flip didn't speak. He didn't need to. Outside, the corn whispered like dry applause. Inside, something had shifted for good.

CHAPTER 14

FIVE MINUTES OUT

Gwendolynn Pen gripped the edge of the toilet seat as if it might hold her to the Earth. Her palms, streaked with sweat and filth, trembled in slow pulses. The dim light above her buzzed, casting her in an unforgiving glare. It hummed like a memory—loud, unceasing, impossible to ignore.

Her overnight bag sat open on the filthy floor beside her, a cheap canvas bag that sagged like her shoulders. Inside: a bent comb, a pack of yellowed tissues at the corners, a cracked compact mirror... and beneath it all, the steel whisper of a stiletto blade. She stared at it. Not touching it. Not yet.

Lance's voice boomed through the bus intercom, crackling over the hum of the diesel. "May I have your attention, please? We are entering the terminal at Gateway City. This is the final destination—"

She pressed her fingers to her ears. Final destination. Her whole body convulsed.

This bus—the scent, the walls, the stall—had been a coffin long before she'd climbed aboard. She wasn't afraid of death. No. That had already happened. Weeks ago, when her son was burned to death in a rollover of a bus on a rain-slick highway outside Gateway City.

The casket had been closed. The driver escaped without being charged. The company settled for less than the cost of burying him.

He'd died on a bus. Now here she sat, trapped in one, heading toward a funeral she could barely afford and a town where no one had been waiting for her.

Her hand reached into the bag. The blade shimmered like a warning. Her thumb touched the spine. Cold. Smooth. Honest.

There had been a time when she read poetry. When she quoted Dickinson to students who scribbled notes with tired eyes. When she bought her son a thesaurus because she said, "Words are bridges, not fences." Now words failed her.

The mirror beside her leg caught a flicker of her reflection. She flipped it over. What was left to say? Her fingers closed around the stiletto. She unsnapped it. The blade popped out in a clean arc. A gentle click followed. Final. Mechanical. As if giving permission. She placed it against her wrist. Her hands shook—but not with fear. With resolve. With something close to stillness. A slow breath entered her lungs. She counted with it. One. Two. Three.

Her gaze fell to the photo, buried between a torn paperback and a cracked travel lotion. Her son. Eight years old. Arms around a fishing pole. Smile too wide for his face. The knife slipped. She lowered it. Her chest hitched. A sob caught in her ribs and refused to rise. Her body hunched. Shoulders caved inward. The stiletto fell into the muck with a muted clink. She cried, pulling the photo to her chest and rocking forward and back, her mouth open in a scream that never escaped her throat.

Time no longer moved. Outside, the bus turned onto the terminal access road.

Inside, grief hollowed her out, slow as acid.

CHAPTER 15

TERMINAL DESCENT

Morgan sits near the back of the bus, arms wrapped tightly around herself. The cold vinyl seats press against her, but the heat of shame pulses under her skin, making the discomfort seem justified. Her reflection flickers in the darkened window, a vague, unfamiliar face that wears a smile too easily, a smile that cuts too deep.

The sound of the bus shifting gears echoed like a growl beneath her feet. They were close now. The road had straightened, and the signs had changed. Gateway City loomed ahead, the destination no longer theoretical.

She hadn't spoken since Mark gutted her with the truth. Cruel fluff. That's what he'd called her. Not bitch. Not whore. That would've been easy to laugh off. But fluff — that was worse. Dismissive. She'd never mattered. A shadow cast by someone else's light.

She crossed her legs and tugged her skirt down, suddenly aware of how short it was and how ridiculous she looked trying to be what men wanted when none of them had stayed.

The silence on the bus had thickened. No more snickering sailors. No more giggles behind cupped hands. Just breathing. Hot metal and road noise.

Morgan's eyes drifted toward the rear and froze. A dark smear trailed from the edge of the toilet door. Thin, deliberate. A slow-moving stain the color of rusted cherries. Her body snapped upright. Blood! She blinked once, twice. No change. It wasn't a thread. It wasn't dirt. It was moving. "Shit..." she whispered. Then a screech. "Driver!"

Lance's eyes widen as her scream pierces the air. Frantically, he slams on the brakes. The bus swerves wildly, tires screeching before it comes to a sudden halt. He springs from his seat and runs down the aisle. Morgan rises quickly, her finger pointing sharply. Her voice cracks like a struck match. "There's blood coming from the John!" The words slice through the cabin, sharp and sudden.

Flip shot up and sprinted to the rear, urgency in his movements. "Move!" he barked at Morgan. She stumbled aside, her hand gripping the rail as Flip shoved against the toilet door. It resisted at first, but he pushed again, and finally it gave way.

Gwendolynn Pen collapsed onto the urine-soaked floor, her body limp. Gasps broke like waves. One passage screamed, another gagged. Lance's knees buckled at the sight. He dropped to the floor beside her, his hands fluttering. He didn't know where to touch. "God, no... Please, no..."

Flip checked her wrist, silence betraying the absence of a pulse. “She’s dead,” he murmured, voice heavy. "She’s gone, Lance." An uneasy stillness settled over the bus.

Morgan pressed her back against the window, sliding down until her cheek rested against the glass. Her mouth parted, but no words came. An eerie silence filled the bus—so still, it was almost deafening.

Lance didn’t move. He stayed crouched, staring at Gwendolynn’s hand. Her fingers still clutched the photo. He reached out and caressed it.

“I wonder if that knife hurt you as much as we did,” he whispered. Mark, standing behind him, closed his eyes and nodded. “We can’t hurt her anymore.”

Outside the bus, the flashing lights of an ambulance danced across the windows. Inside, guilt pressed against every ribcage. And no one—not Flip, not Mark, not even Morgan—dared speak a word.

CHAPTER 16

NOT GARBAGE

The ambulance idled beside the bus, as if waiting for trash pickup.

The two EMTs boarded with the detachment of janitors on overtime — starched uniforms, rubber gloves, and a black vinyl body bag dangling from the hand of a tall, lanky man like laundry.

The older EMT, with tired eyes and too many memories, knelt beside Gwendolynn and checked for a pulse, more ritual than concern. He nodded to his partner. The second EMT rolled out the body bag and pulled the zipper down, the teeth spreading like a grin. Plastic crinkled. The sound turned Lance's stomach.

"What's that?" Lance asked. The attendant didn't look up. "Body bag." Lance rose slowly, his knees popping. His hand clutched the pole beside him, white-knuckled. "No," he said. The attendant blinked. "Sir—" "She didn't come on this bus like no sack of garbage," Lance growled. "And she ain't leaving it like one."

The tall attendant straightened, uncertain. "Protocol says—" "I don't give a damn about protocol." Lance's voice dropped, gravel-thick. "You think that's all she is? Something to zip up and toss into a van?" The first attendant hesitated. "She's deceased. We're here to—" "To clean up. Yeah, I get it."

Lance stepped over the threshold between the aisle and Gwendolynn's body. His arms reached down and slid beneath her knees and shoulders. She weighed so little, it frightened him. Paper-thin. Bird-light. As if the world had been carving pieces off her for years. He held her against his chest. Death had stolen her smile. Now only a blank stare. Was she seeing her son Duncan? Or maybe I had changed — his senses calibrated to something deeper than odor.

Flip moved to his side without a word. So did Mark. "Let's go," Lance said. He took the first step down the bus stairs. At the base of the steps, the younger EMT started to protest. "You really want to pick her up?" he asked, eyes flicking to the spot of blood on her shirt. "She might have AIDS." Lance paused. His jaw flexed. His gaze cut through the boy like a scalpel. "I don't care," he said softly. "Chivalry ain't dead."

He walked through the heat of the long night into the cool terminal's air conditioning, Gwendolynn's body in his arms, her photograph still clutched between her stiffening fingers. Passengers stared through the glass as they got off the bus. None of them said a word.

Lance didn't ask for help. He didn't need to. He'd already done what mattered.He'd seen her. And she would not be garbage.

CHAPTER 17

DIRTY JUSTICE

The inside of the bus stank even worse now. Not from the toilet — though that reek still clung to the walls like mildew — but from something deeper, heavier. Shame.

Flip McCracken sat on the edge of his seat, elbows on his knees, eyes fixed on the spot where Gwendolynn had collapsed. The smear of blood hadn't been cleaned. Neither had the silence. Everyone on that bus had watched her unravel. No one had moved until it was too late. Except Lance.

Flip rubbed his palms together slowly, his jaw clenched. Across the aisle, Antony stretched lazily, his eyes cold and unrepentant. His lips curled into a self-satisfied grin, as if he'd gotten away with something.

"Hey," Antony muttered to no one in particular. "She probably planned that whole damn thing. Get a little attention. Women love that."

Flip turned. "You want to repeat that?" Antony glanced at him, a smirk rising like steam. "Relax, old man. Ain't nobody died from being ugly. Crazy bitch did what crazy bitches do."Flip stood. Mark stood with him.

The bus no longer moved, but its frame shuddered. Antony shifted in his seat, the edge of confidence beginning to slip. "What the hell is this?" The stern faces of Flip and Mark stared back. "You want to talk trash?" Mark said, voice low and solid. "Let's take it where it belongs." Flip grabbed Antony by the collar before he could twitch. Mark twisted the sailor's arm behind his back. Together, they hauled him down the aisle like a bag of spoiled meat.

"No!" Antony shouted. "What the fuck! Get off me—" The toilet door yawned open. Flip shoved it wide. The stench hit like a slap. "Wait—wait! You crazy bastards—" Mark flung the stall wide. Flip kicked Antony's legs out. He dropped with a thud. His arms flailed. Flip shoved his head forward—into the overstuffed toilet bowl, into the filth, the rot, the stinging ghost of everything he'd laughed at. Antony screamed—a wet, muffled wail.

The bus shook with rage; it shook with failure. Flip pulled him up by the shirt, let him cough, and let the smell soak into his pristine white uniform. "Now," Flip said, almost gently, "you smell like your soul." He let go.

Antony crumpled to the floor, puking, shirt stained brown and yellow. Mark stared down at him, disgust and disappointment locked behind his eyes. Flip turned and walked away. Behind him, the stall door creaked shut. Justice didn't always come clean. Sometimes, it came covered in everything you deserved.

CHAPTER 18

SPOILED MEAT

Morgan Wright, her arms folded like bars across her chest. Her reflection in the smeared window glass rippled each time the bus lights flickered.

The silence pressed in. Not quite silence. Hollow, stifling, like the space inside a coffin before the dirt hits. No one looked at her. No one flirted. No one laughed at her jokes.

Her blouse still hung just right, her lipstick unbothered. But none of it mattered now. Not after the blood. Not after the mirror. Not after Lance carried that woman like something precious, while Morgan had done nothing but spit venom at her.

Cruel fluff.

That's what Mark had said. "There's not even a real person. Just make-believe." It had hit harder than any slap.

She'd spent years perfecting the act — the strut, the pout, the come-hither curves. She was the girl you wanted to take to bed but not bring home. The one with the sharp tongue and a hard edge. It kept her safe, or so she'd thought.

Now it felt like a costume that didn't fit anymore.

Antony sat two rows ahead, still hunched, still reeking of humiliation and raw sewage. No one sat near him. His pride had dissolved in that toilet bowl, and Morgan couldn't summon the energy to gloat. She wasn't better. She wasn't anything.

She pressed her forehead to the cool glass. In the faint reflection, she saw herself again — but behind her own image, ghostly, was Gwendolynn.

The old woman's eyes hadn't pleaded. They hadn't even looked angry. Just... tired. She'd seen every cruelty this world had to offer and still somehow kept breathing. Until now. Morgan closed her eyes.

Her mother had always said, "Pretty only lasts until someone looks closer."

She opened her purse. Dug through it, maybe a different woman was hiding inside. Gum, lipstick, a travel-sized perfume bottle. Shallow things. Hollow things. No mirror. No damn mirror.

Mark had stopped looking at her. Not like a man who'd lost interest — like someone who'd finally seen what was behind the curtain and wished he hadn't looked.

"I didn't mean it," she whispered, barely audible. No one heard her. That was the real punishment. She'd been loud all day, strutting, owning the aisle. And now her apology was too quiet, too late.

Morgan sank into her seat, her arms relaxing and her legs folding in. For the first time in years, she looked genuinely small—like a girl, not a tease or a brat. Just a seventeen-year-old who had watched someone die and understood she had played a part in it.

Spoiled meat. Lance had called the passengers earlier. Morgan understood now. You rot from the inside, and you don't even notice until the stench chokes everyone around you. She didn't cry. Tears would've made it about her again. Instead, she sat still, silent, and let it hurt.

CHAPTER 19

THE LEATHER CASE

The last passenger had wandered off into the terminal's fluorescent arms. Flip sat outside, smoking. Antony huddled at the back of the bus, reeking and silent. Morgan hadn't moved in twenty minutes.

Lance Avery returned to the bus and shut off the engine. The world fell silent. He turned slowly toward the worn leather overnight case abandoned on the toilet floor—still buckled, scuffed at the corners, as if it had seen more life than most people ever would. He reached for it. His fingers trembled, not with fear, but with reverence.

Gwendolynn had clutched that bag. She had slept with it pressed to her chest, defended it, Shielded it. And, it witnessed her last breath. Lance opened the latches, one at a time. Metal clicked softly, sharp in the still air. Inside, the first thing he saw was the knife. A stiletto.

Not hidden. Not sheathed. Just lying atop the other contents like a discarded secret. Dried blood kissed the edge. Not much.

But enough to whisper what she had almost done—and what she finally had.

He swallowed and set the knife aside with care.

Below it, folded tightly, were worn pajamas, yellowed from years. They smelled of lavender and stale cigarettes. A toothbrush. A funeral program, folded in half, creased with worry and tears.

And at the bottom — a photograph. A boy, maybe twenty, in a powder blue cap and gown. An arm slung around Gwendolynn's shoulders. Both smiling. No, grinning. Pure joy bursting through the photo paper. Their hands linked at the center, like a bond nothing could break. Except a bus.

Lance turned the photo over. Scrawled on the back in crooked handwriting: **"My baby. My everything. Duncan Pen, 1984–2006."** A date. A name. No explanation. But he didn't need one.

Lance pressed the photo flat against his palm and closed his eyes. This wasn't a homeless woman. This wasn't a crazy woman. This wasn't meat. This was a mother heading to bury her son—the same way Lance had buried pieces of himself after that strike, after the betrayal, after losing faith in people.

His hands searched the bag, settling on a single piece of paper, crumpled to the point of dissolving. A bus ticket. Chicago to Gateway City. Paid in cash. No return. No round-trip. Lance folded the ticket, set the photo beside it, and closed the bag carefully—like tucking someone in for the last time.

He sat still. The grief came, not like a storm but like water soaking into old wood—slow, creeping, irreversible. He picked up the microphone. Not to make an announcement. Not yet. Instead, he looked out through the windshield at the ghost-lit terminal and whispered, "I'm sorry, Duncan. She got there. But not the way she should have."

His voice cracked. "She should've had flowers. A seat near the window. Someone waiting on the other side." He held the overnight case like a relic, not cargo.

"She shouldn't have gone out like that. For the first time since the strike, since the company gutted him like livestock, Lance remembered what it meant to carry something cherished."

CHAPTER 20

THE REAL ARRIVAL

Lance stepped from the bus, Gwendolynn Pen's lifeless body cradled in his arms.

The night clung to Gateway City's terminal like old chewing gum — gray, cold, and tasteless.

No one saw him at first. No one paid attention. There was no fanfare, no procession, no hush of reverence. Only gum-smacking janitors, flickering vending machines, and the faint buzz of fluorescent light.

Lance continued his steady pace, each boot meeting the linoleum with a measured, deliberate strike. The sound reverberated loudly, filling the space with a weight that felt far too pronounced for mere footsteps.

Flip was the first to notice him, rising abruptly from a bench near the vending machines. The cigarette in his hand slipped free as he straightened up, his eyes widening—not with shock, but with awe. Mark followed quietly behind, silent and reverent.

Lance didn't meet their eyes. His gaze was fixed forward, pinned to a point past the ticket counters and lost schedules. He wasn't carrying weight anymore. He was carrying a truth. People started turning. Heads lifted. Whispers stuttered through the crowd. "Is that a...?" "Is she dead?" "What's he doing?"

No one moved to stop him. Not even the uniformed transit worker by the entrance, who backed up two steps like Lance's grief radiated heat.

The security guard near the station's side door lifted his walkie-talkie halfway, hesitated, then lowered it again. Lance moved to the center of the terminal and stopped. He surveyed his surroundings. No podium, no church pews, no priest—only this space had become her sanctuary.

"I won't let them bag her," Lance said quietly, to no one and everyone. "She's not trash." Flip approached slowly. His voice came tight, like he was swallowing something sharp. "Lance. You want me to—?" Lance shook his head. "She made it to her boy. One way or another." Mark stood a few feet off, hands at his sides, like a sailor not sure if he was still under orders. Lance knelt. Gently, he laid her on a bench, not like luggage or loss, but like something precious that needed to rest.

He opened the overnight case, pulled out the photo of Duncan Pen, and tucked it beneath her folded hands. He didn't need tape. The pose held. The quiet that followed was the kind reserved for cathedrals and crumbling hearts.

Flip cleared his throat loudly enough for all to hear. "She was somebody," Mark interjected. "She was a mother." A brief pause.

Then a voice from across the station broke through. Morgan's voice: "She didn't deserve what we gave her." Morgan stood stiff, mascara streaked, her voice thin but firm. She walked forward, out of the shadows of her own cruelty. Lance looked up at her. Nodded once. She nodded back. Heads turned.

The station manager approached, clipboard in hand, but hesitated at the edge of the group. "Is... there anything we should... do?" Lance rose, slow and solid. "You can wait," he said.

The station manager blinked. "Wait?" Lance picked up the overnight case. "Yeah. Until someone from her family comes. Or until a proper ride arrives. But she doesn't leave this bench in a bag."

The station manager looked around, meeting the eyes of Mark, Flip, Morgan—even Antony, still filthy and silent at the periphery. He nodded once. Quietly. "All right." Lance turned to Flip. "I'm off the clock." "You damn right," Flip muttered, his throat closing. Together, they stood in a makeshift vigil. Not for a stranger. For a woman who deserved more.

CHAPTER 21

THE THING ABOUT SHAME

Morgan Wright sat alone in the terminal bathroom, staring at her reflection in the cracked mirror, bloodshot eyes staring back, mascara smeared. The fluorescent light buzzed overhead, its hum almost nervous, mingling with the distant flushing toilets and whirring hand dryers. She looked tired, unglamorous, far from star-bound. Just a girl who'd kicked a woman as she crawled toward her son's grave. She dabbed under her eyes with a paper towel, tore it, tried again.

In the stall behind her, someone flushed. The sound made her flinch. She'd laughed at the smell. The way she laughed and mocked Gwendolynn in the toilet on the bus. Called her names like it was nothing—like pain was something you could judge by smell and hair and dirty fingernails.

"She ain't nobody." Morgan had said that. She lied to herself so thoroughly that it came out smooth. She threw the ruined paper towel in the trash and walked out of the restroom, eyes lowered, shoulders tight. She didn't want attention. Not tonight.

The bench still supported Gwendolynn's body, a folded transit blanket draped over her like a shroud. Flip stood nearby, arms crossed, watching over her like a brother at a funeral. Lance and Mark were nowhere in sight.

Antony hunched beside the vending machine, dirt caked into his skin. His arms were crossed tightly, and he hadn't budged since being dragged off the bus. The stench of his uniform kept everyone at least ten feet away.

Morgan approached slowly, her boots clicking on the tile. Antony glanced at her, sneering. "Well, if it isn't Hollywood. You come to sign autographs?" Morgan didn't smile. Didn't joke. Didn't sway her hips or toss her hair. She looked at him—through him—and said, "We did that."

Antony blinked. "What?" "We killed her." His eyes narrowed. "Don't go poetic on me now. She offed herself." Morgan's voice cracked like brittle paper. "She climbed into that toilet to hide from us, Antony. From you. From me."

Antony shrugged, his body shifting in the seat. "She was nuts. Don't pin that shit on me." Morgan leaned in close, her words sharp, quiet, and hot. "She had a son. Did you hear that? A son she was burying. And all we saw was a mess to mock. That makes us worse than the stink, Antony. Worse than the piss. At least that didn't have a choice." Antony's lip curled, but he didn't speak.

Morgan took a step back, her hands trembling openly. "You think you're tough," she whispered, a tremor in her voice. "But you're just small. Same as me." Without another word, she turned and headed toward the bench.

Gwendolynn didn't look peaceful. Death hadn't smoothed her wrinkles or softened her brow. But Morgan knelt beside her. Not for show. Not for drama. Because shame needed a witness.

Morgan's hand slipped into her coat pocket, retrieving a coral pink lipstick—the shade she believed made her stand out. She set it delicately on the bench beside the photo of Duncan, an insignificant gesture yet personal. Without a word, she faced Antony, her eyes steady. "You should apologize before your tongue rots out of your head," she declared. Turning sharply, she walked away, her footsteps leaving a heavy silence behind.

CHAPTER 22

FLIP'S FAREWELL

The wheeled gurney squeaked as it entered the terminal. Two ambulance attendants, clipboard and gloves in hand, came through the sliding glass doors with calm faces. Flip McCracken stood from his spot near the bench and straightened his coat. He didn't speak. Didn't wave them over. Just stared until they met his eyes. One of the attendants gave a half-nod. Flip didn't return it. He stepped between them and the body. "No bag."

The taller EMT blinked. "Excuse me?" "You heard me," Flip said. "No body bag. You cover her, you carry her, you treat her like you'd treat your own mother if she went quiet on a bus bench."

The second EMT, the younger one, glanced toward the terminal manager, who hovered near the ticket kiosk, pretending to read a brochure. No help there.

"She's—uh—deceased, sir." "You don't say," Flip growled. "And she's also human. So unless your paperwork says 'dispose of like biohazard,' you can drop the zipper and pick up the respect."

There was a pause. One of those pauses when someone younger realizes the man barking at them isn't bluffing. Slowly, the attendants folded the black bag back into their cart.

Flip stepped aside. "Thank you," he said quietly. "She's ready now." Together, they lifted Gwendolynn Pen—wrapped in the thin transit blanket, photo of Duncan pressed to her chest—and placed her on the stretcher. The room shifted. Something heavy passed through the space, like gravity remembered its job.

Morgan stood nearby, arms wrapped around herself. Mark leaned against a column, head bowed. Antony—filthy, small, beaten by silence—sat, and didn't crack a joke.

Flip followed the stretcher to the door. He stopped at the threshold, looked back at the bench and the overnight case, still sitting like a relic no one dared touch. He spoke, low and to himself. "Good gosh, baby... the world don't deserve some people." No one heard it. Didn't matter.

Flip turned toward the terminal exit, his steps slowing as he reached into his jacket pocket for a wrapped candy bar. He carried it to the bench and set it beside the case—his only offering. He glanced back at the ambulance, took a final breath, and whispered softly, "Tell your boy we're sorry." The ambulance disappeared into the night, carrying Gwendolynn this time with deliberate care.

CHAPTER 23

ONE MORE STOP

The engine hummed low, steady, like a creature catching its breath.

Lance Avery sat alone in the driver's seat, elbows propped on the wheel. The dashboard clock ticked louder than it should have. Outside, the terminal lights buzzed with an incandescent glow, hazy through the windshield's greasy streaks.

The ambulance had gone. The body was gone. But the weight hadn't lifted.

He looked in the rearview mirror at the aisle that now carried the memory of her — a broken woman who had asked for nothing more than silence, and even that had been stolen from her.

No one had claimed the overnight bag. No one would. Gwendolynn Pen was no one's burden now. Not a mother. Not a friend. Not even a ghost to most.

Lance reached out and picked up the small mirror she'd left behind. Cracked. Cheap. The kind of thing you got at a five-and-dime when you couldn't afford dignity. He turned it in his hands. How many times had she stared into it, trying to find something left to fix?

"She had a son," he said aloud. The bus didn't answer. "Going to school, or was it a funeral?" He sighed, his jaw tightening. "Doesn't matter. Either way, she was going toward something. And we... we didn't even ask her name until it was printed on a tag."

He opened the glove box and tucked the mirror inside; it deserved a place where things were kept safe.

Flip stepped aboard quietly, his shoes scraping the steps. "You alright?" Flip asked. "No," Lance replied. That was expected. Flip nodded. "You did right." Lance shook his head. "Too late." "Still right." Silence stretched between them like a tightrope.

"I was going to quit," Lance said finally. "After this run. Turn in the keys. Let someone else haul the meat." Flip looked at him carefully. "Still going to?" Lance glanced toward the terminal. "No. Not yet." "Why not?" "Because she didn't make it." Flip folded his arms. "Somebody's got to stay behind and give a damn."Lance said.

The air conditioner kicked on with a rattle, pushing the stink around instead of clearing it. But Lance didn't mind it anymore.

It reminded him of what happens when no one speaks up. When no one sees the person behind the smell, behind the clothes, behind the silence. "She was afraid of buses," Lance whispered. "And she got on anyway." Flip said nothing. What was there to say?

Outside, a few terminal workers walked by, laughing about something trivial, unaware of the funeral that had passed right under their noses.

Lance adjusted his mirror, hands steady now. The job wasn't done. There was still one more stop to make.

CHAPTER 24

NO ROUND TRIP

Lance Avery eased the bus into the depot garage with a calm that unsettled the mechanics. He didn't slam the brakes or bark into the intercom. He simply parked, leaned forward and flipped the switch shut off the engine and killed the lights. He sat behind the wheel like a priest in an empty confessional.

A few feet away, a red-eyed dispatcher tapped her clipboard against her thigh. "Long trip?" she asked. Lance didn't respond. He was still watching the front seat. It was empty now, but he saw her ghost in it. Gwendolynn Pen. Arms wrapped around a scuffed leather case. Eyes gaunt, too deep. A laugh that didn't fit the pain it covered.

He finally stood, his knees cracking. His back relaxed, and he moved with deliberate confidence—no longer a cargo hauler or meat pusher, just a human. The dispatcher, reading the pain on his face, spoke. "Any incidents?" Lance considered it. "No," he said. "Just life."

He stepped off the bus and made his way to the locker room. With deliberate care, he changed out of his uniform, folding each piece meticulously. He placed his cap on top of the stack. Now it held some unspoken significance.

He walked through the lot toward the parking area, Flip leaning against a post, smoking silently. Neither spoke. Under the buzzing floodlight that flickered like a distant memory, they stood in silence, avoiding each other's gaze.

Lance broke the silence. "She had one of those graduation photos in her bag." Flip exhaled slowly. "Duncan?" Lance nodded. "Nineteen. Dead in a crash. This bus line." Flip flinched like it caught him in the ribs. "Shit."

"She was headed to his funeral. Alone. Scared. Surrounded by jackals." He didn't have to say names. They both knew. Flip dropped the cigarette and crushed it under his heel. Lance watched the smoke curl up from the pavement. "You know what I kept thinking?" "What's that?" "She didn't buy a round-trip ticket. One-way. Cash." Flip nodded. "No round trip," he murmured. "That says it."

Lance turned to him. "We keep saying people are meat, Flip. From point A to point B. But maybe they're not. Maybe they're stories. And we're the pages they land on—just long enough to leave a mark."

Flip rubbed the back of his neck. "You quitting?" Lance shook his head. "I'm driving again tomorrow." Flip raised an eyebrow. "Why?"

"Because somebody's gotta see them. Not inspect. Not judge. *See.*" Flip smiled. Not wide. Not smug. But real. "You gonna make a habit of picking up the broken ones?" Lance's mouth twitched. "Maybe."

He started his car. The sky had softened at the edges—purple bruises giving way to early morning gold. The kind of light that doesn't ask for forgiveness, only offers it.

Lance looked over his shoulder. A gentle, warm breeze brushed his face. "Hey, Flip?" "Yeah?" he smiled. "Next time someone stinks up your bus, maybe don't turn your nose up. Maybe ask their name." Flip lowered his head and chuckled, then lazily saluted. "Yes, Captain Chivalry." Lance grinned and drove off into the rising heat of a new day. No radio. No passengers. Just quiet. For the first time in years, he didn't hate it.

ABOUT THE AUTHOR

S.J. Rogers is a Chicago-born writer whose work is rooted in discipline, perseverance, and lived experience. He discovered writing while serving in the U.S. Navy, where storytelling became both craft and calling. After a decade of service, Rogers worked across transportation and logistics industries while pursuing higher education. In midlife, he confronted and overcame dyslexia, sharpening his voice through formal study. His writing reflects decades of observation and a belief that meaningful stories are forged through endurance, curiosity, and respect for the written word.

www.ingramcontent.com/pod-product-compliance
Lightning Source LLC
LaVergne TN
LVHW010837120826
845149LV00017B/1482

* 9 7 9 8 9 9 4 8 5 7 0 1 4 *